For Luka and Ollie; love Dad x

Text Copyright:
Andrew Shaw

Illustration Copyright:
Andrew Shaw

Book Illustrations by:
Daamouche Mohamed

ISBN 978-0-646-83108-4 (paperback)
Published by AndrewShawBooks
www.andrewshawbooks.com

BRIAN THE BARRACUDA

Written by Andrew Shaw

Brian the barracuda,
He swims the seven seas,
He's often looking for a friend,
He always aims to please!

He tries to be so friendly,
His smile he likes to show,
But no matter what he does,
The fish don't want to know!

Brian always wants to play,
But sometimes gets confused,
He often turns up unannounced,
The others look bemused!

The fish all leave so quickly,
Their tails are in his face,
Brian thinks it is a game,
And treats it like a race!

But the other fish aren't playing,
They swim away and hide,
All the fish are scared of him,
They all look terrified!

Brian does not understand,
Why do they swim away?
He's well dressed and approachable,
But no one wants to play!

And Brian is determined now,
To find out why they leave,
He makes a plan to ask around,
The truth he must achieve!

So he straightens up his tie,
And sets off for the truth,
He sees a big shark sleeping there,
He's feeling bulletproof!

Brian moves toward the shark,
His smile is quite supreme,
The shark takes one quick look at him,
And lets out a big scream!

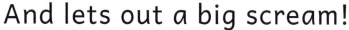

Before he can say hello,
The shark is up and gone,
It speeds off like a submarine,
He knows he should move on!

After swimming through the rocks,
Determined not to fail,
Brian finds another fish,
And swims toward a whale!

Brian tries to play it cool,
Well-mannered, he says please,
Brian looks him in the eye,
His breath blows in the breeze!

The whale then stares right back at him,
Its eyes and face turn red,
Brian's breath goes up his nose,
And flows straight to his head!

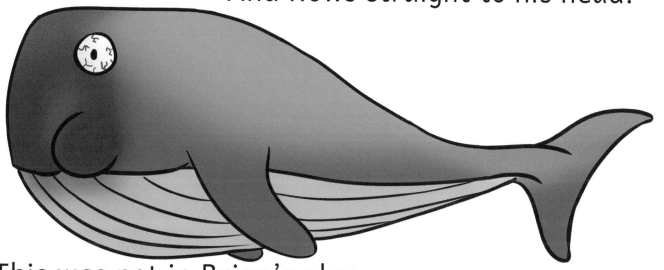

This was not in Brian's plan,
Which clearly is in doubt,
But before he speaks again,
The big whale passes out!

"It isn't looking good for me,
I'll give it one last go,
Clearly big fish can't help me,
The small fish, they may know!"

The smaller fish are hard to find,
He checks in the seaweed,
He sees a sardine hiding there,
And Brian starts to plead ...

"Why do they all swim away?
It really makes me sad!
It's something I don't understand,
I hope I'm not that bad!"

The sardine knows he needs some help,
He's daunted by his task,
He reaches deep inside his pouch,
And grabs a snorkel mask!

"Okay, I will tell you why,
I don't want to be mean,
The reason why you scare them off,
Your teeth are never clean!"

"Your breath it smells like stinky socks,
It's well known in the reef,
Your mouth is filled with lots of food,
There's bits stuck in your teeth!"

"Come with me!" the sardine smiled,
I'll show you what I see,"
A mirror lay beneath the sand,
"Please look at this for me!"

Brian looks into the glass,
His teeth are quite a sight,
Food is hanging everywhere,
It gives him quite a fright!

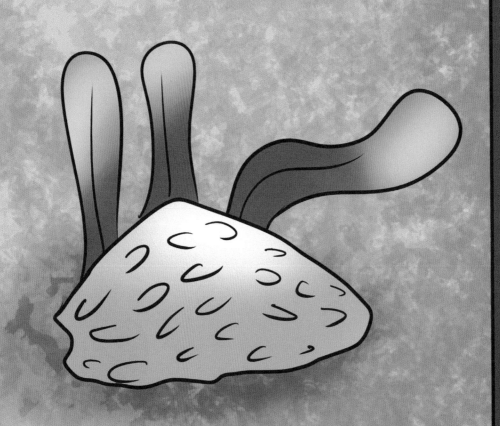

"Have you ever cleaned your teeth?
I know where you should go!
There is a dentist down the coast,
Next to the salmon roe!"

Brian thanked his new best friend,
Then swam to get some help,
He went straight to the dentist's room,
And waited with some kelp!

The dentist welcomed Brian in,
Her calming voice a plus,
Brian was surprised to see,
A friendly octopus!

1

"First of all you take your brush,
And then add some toothpaste,
Then the brush goes in your mouth,
And on your teeth it's placed!"

2

3

"Brush up high and brush down low,
Be sure to clean them all,
Take your time and do not rush,
The germs are very small!"

④

"If you do not brush your teeth,
The germs will start to spread,
Your breath will smell, your teeth will ache,
Your mouth will soon be red!"

⑤

⑥

2 MINUTES +

"If you do this every day,
The germs will take a hike,
Do this for two minutes please,
Or longer if you like!"

The dentist cleaned all Brian's teeth,
A smile now on his lips,
She also took out all the food,
Some seaweed and some chips!

"Thank you, miss," young Brian beams,
"I don't know what to say?"
"Here's a gift ... your own toothbrush,
Please use it twice a day!"

Brian left excitedly,
His smile is big and bright,
His teeth are lighting up the reef,
He swims with all his might!

Brian's smile shines far and wide,
The squid feel out of tune,
It messes up their body clocks,
They think he is the moon!

His teeth are now so sparkly white,
His breath no longer green,

He is the new talk of the reef,
Including the sea bream!

All the fish now follow him,
They plan for their weekend!
"Will you come and swim with us?"
They want to be his friend!

Brian is so handsome now,
Some others have a crush,
His life has now completely changed,
All thanks to a toothbrush!

And Brian now has lots of friends,
The tide has turned for him!
The fish all line up at his door,
And ask him for a swim!

"Will you come and swim with us?
We will explore the reef!"

"Just give me two more minutes please ...
I need to brush my teeth!"

Printed in Great Britain
by Amazon